Maylan Schurch

The Sky-High Mystery

REVIEW AND HERALD® PUBLISHING ASSOCIATION
HAGERSTOWN, MD 21740

This book was
Edited by Randy Fishell
Copyedited by James Cavil
Cover designed by Pierce Creative
Cover illustration by Thompson Brothers/Del Thompson
Interior design by Candy Harvey
Electronic makeup by Shirley M. Bolivar
Typeset: 10.5/14 Cheltenham

PRINTED IN U.S.A.

09 08 07 06 05 5 4 3 2 1

R&H Cataloging Service
Schurch, Maylan Henry, 1950- .
The sky-high mystery.

I. Title.

813.6

ISBN 0-8280-1867-7

Dedication

To Shelley—
my cosurvivor of our five-mile
trek to the Dungeness Spit
lighthouse in Sequim, Washington.

Acknowledgments

Thank you, veteran pilots Tom Claps and Herb Brown, for the inspiration you've given me. Tom, I'll never forget the tumbling (but tightly controlled) ride you gave me in your aerobatic biplane *Eagle*. Herb, thank you for joining Tom on the platform as I interviewed you both during a Sabbath sermon on faith—and for telling the story of your emergency landing on a Seattle softball field during a game!

Thank you, Nedra Leriget, for letting me use your computer and the peace and quiet of your Kansas City home to start this book during the vacation visit your sister (my wife) and I made there.

Other books by Maylan Schurch:

Justin Case Adventures

1. *The Case of the Stolen Red Mary*
2. *The Desert Temple Mystery*
3. *Danger Signals in Belize*
4. *Trouble in Masai Mara*
5. *The Meatless Mayhem Mystery*

Beware of the Crystal Dragon

Blinded by the Light

The Great Graffiti Mystery

The Rapture

Rescue From Beyond Orion

A Thousand Shall Fall

Contents

One

Hideout on Wheels

"One more game," Gina commanded. Expertly shuffling the pack of Dutch Blitz cards, she began to deal them onto the carpet.

Thirteen-year-old Justin Case groaned. "You said that five games ago."

"What's the matter?" She gathered up her cards, squared the deck, and grinned at him. "Don't you like Dutch Blitz?"

"I liked it better 20 games ago," Justin replied.

"We haven't played 20 games, just eight. Ready? *Go!"* She started slapping down her cards, which had numbers and pictures of little Dutch boys and girls on them.

Justin glanced around at the long black leather seat that ran along one side of the car. He glanced at the polished wood refreshment rack just below the opposite window, which held his can of Sprite. He glanced at his new friend Gina Coggins, who sat cross-legged on the plush velvet carpet facing him, holding the pack of cards.

"Come on," she said. "Play."

"Gina, stop."

"Why?"

"I'm bored."

Gina slapped down three more cards. "What do you think *I* am?"

"You're bored?"

"Play," she said. "You're the one who invited me along on this limo ride."

"Look, Gina—" Justin began.

The girl sighed and tossed the rest of her cards on the carpet. "When you talked me into coming along, I thought we were just going to glide through town, sipping our Sprites and enjoying the view of the bay."

"Gina—"

"But what happens? Your brother drives two blocks and pulls up in front of a restaurant and goes in. Five minutes later he comes out and drives another block to another restaurant, and goes in. The same thing happens again and again and again. What kind of fun is that? I could have stayed home and answered my e-mail." She scowled. "It's lucky I had these Dutch Blitz cards in my backpack."

"Gina, Robbie's *got* to stop every couple of blocks. Your dad got him the limo-driver job so he could work part-time while he's going to college here."

"I know that."

"So Robbie's stopping at restaurants and

hotels and giving them his business card, and asking them to put it on their bulletin boards. Otherwise how's anybody going to know he's in the limo business?"

"OK, fine," the girl said. "But why did *we* have to come along?"

"Robbie's taking us out to lunch with him. At the Mongolian Grill."

"Oh." Gina sounded impressed. "Well, in that case . . . But I'm still bored." She fixed a glittering eye on Justin. "And I still want to know why we had to come along," she repeated. "Answer my question, or we have to play another game."

Justin's attention was distracted by a distant shout. Looking through the limo's tinted glass, which made everything outside look grayish, he noticed four or five boys on a street corner a block away. They seemed to be harassing another boy about Justin's age. The boy was backing quickly away from the kids and toward the limo.

"What?" Justin asked vaguely. "What question?"

"What's the *real* reason you've got us trapped in this limo on a sunny day?"

"Look at those kids," he said. "They're getting into a fight."

"Answer me."

"No, look. Down the block there."

Gina's gaze followed his pointing finger.

Suddenly she was up on her knees on the long leather seat, her eyes wide, her forehead pressed against the glass. "Tony!" she squealed. "That's Tony!"

"That's your brother?" Justin asked. "I thought he was at camp."

"He *is* at camp," she said, staring hard. "At least he's supposed to be."

Justin watched the kids. "Which one is he?"

"*You* know Tony. No, wait, you don't. You just got here yesterday."

"Is he the one they're harassing?" Justin guessed.

"Yes," she said in a worried voice. "We've got to do something."

Tony stopped backing up, turned his back on the kids, and began jogging toward the limo. Justin could see that he was wearing a black beret and an olive-green T-shirt with writing on it.

"Gina." Justin fumbled with the limo's side door handle. "See if you can get his attention. He can dive in here."

Justin opened the door a few inches, and Gina called out, "Tony! In here!"

Tony didn't stop running, but his head swiveled from side to side, searching for the familiar voice.

"Here!" Gina stuck out her hand and waved it madly at him, and he spotted her. The boy's eyes got huge and questioning, but he raced for the limo. His sister swung the door wide and ducked out of the way. Tony tumbled in, and Justin slammed the door and pushed the lock button.

Tony rolled over and got up on his knees. "Lock that door!" he said.

"I did," Justin reassured him.

The three of them watched the boys coming up the street. They weren't running anymore, just looking around, confused.

Gina giggled. "It all happened so fast that they don't know where you are. At least I hope they don't."

Her brother stared at her. "Well, where *am* I?" he asked. "Gina, why are you in a limo?" He swiveled his stare to Justin. "Who are you?"

"Shhhhh!" Gina hissed. "They're coming this way. One of them must have seen you dive in here after all."

Tony flattened himself on the carpet.

"The glass is tinted like a one-way mirror," Justin reassured him. "All they see is their own reflection."

The kids were circling the limo. One of them kicked a tire. A couple of them looked into the driver's compartment, which was separate from where Justin and his new friends were. Two more cupped their hands on either side of their eyes and put their faces against the glass of the passenger area. Justin, Tony, and Gina held their breath as the kids' eyes moved back and forth.

"Hey, Bible-thumper!" one of them shouted. "We know you're in there!"

Two

BREAK-IN!

Suddenly the pursuers scattered, because Justin's brother Robbie had emerged from the restaurant. He was wearing a crisp white shirt, black tie, creased black slacks and a black chauffeur's cap. The driver's door opened with an elegant *click,* and the powerful engine rumbled to life. The limousine glided forward.

"That's my brother Robbie," Justin told Tony.

"And this is Justin," Gina said.

"Oh, *you're* Justin," Tony said. The puzzled look on his face vanished. "Your brother's starting his freshman year at Port Bradley College. Our dad knows your dad. They were police officers together once. And you're staying with us for a week to be with your brother while he gets used to college."

Justin grinned and nodded. "And you've never met me, because I just got here yesterday. And *you've* been at camp." He took a closer look at Tony. The boy had a thin white face and large eyes. Printed on his T-shirt were three Hebrew letters with the words "Israeli

Defense Force" directly underneath them.

"Ahem." Gina cleared her throat menacingly.

"What's up with this limo?" Tony asked.

"Robbie's driving it part-time to help pay his college tuition," Justin explained. "Your dad got him the job."

"Cool," Tony said. "By the way, Dad told me that when you got here he was going to take you flying in the *Bomber* with him."

Justin shuddered. "Um, yeah," he said politely. "He mentioned it."

Gina pounced. "Aha!" she said. *"That's* why you wanted this limo ride so much, Justin. It's an excuse to get out of going up in the *Bomber."* She locked eyes with him. "Is that it?"

Justin nodded, blushing. "I get sick on airplanes."

"And talking about wiggling out of things, Tony," she continued. *"Ahem."*

Tony glanced at her. "Ahem?" he asked.

"You know what I'm 'aheming' about," she said in a level voice.

"What?"

"Why aren't you at Bible camp?"

He shrugged. "Oh, that. I got excused."

Gina frowned suspiciously. "Excused? Do Mom and Dad know?"

"Yep. I got a ride back early so I could help Prof. McAndry get the lighthouse ready for this

Sunday." Tony paused and glanced at Justin again. He reached in his back pocket and brought out a little booklet about the size of a Dutch Blitz card.

His sister rolled her eyes. "Tony, not now."

He ignored her and opened the booklet. "Have you ever wondered," he asked Justin, "where you would spend eternity if you died?"

"Tony, Justin's already a Christian," his sister said.

Tony studied Justin's face for a moment. "You're really saved?"

Justin's ears got a little warm, but he nodded.

"Well, have you prayed the sinner's prayer?"

"Tony," Gina said. "Leave him alone."

Tony ignored her. "So you've asked Jesus into your heart? You've let Him be your Savior and the Lord of your life?"

Justin nodded again.

"All right!" Tony sighed with relief. "You're on our side! Now let me tell you what we've got to do." From his left jeans pocket he pulled a fat wad of folded white paper. A floppy disk fell out of it and landed on the limo's thick carpeting.

A loud, snarling buzz sounded overhead.

"Hey," Gina said with a surprised smile, "that's Dad in the *Bomber!*"

Tony frowned. "Dad's flying too low," he said. "One of these days he's gonna get in trouble."

Still holding the wad of paper, Tony rolled over on his back and stared through the gray window glass at the biplane tumbling through the sky. "You know what's going to happen to that plane when the rapture hits, don't you?"

"Tony," Gina moaned, "do we always have to talk about the rapture?"

Justin glanced out the window. "Hey, we're here," he said. "The Mongolian Grill."

Tony's eyes lit up. He quickly picked up the disk and inserted it back into the wad of paper, and shoved the wad back into his pocket.

Gina looked at him curiously. "Are you hungry?"

Her brother nodded.

"The only problem is," she told him, "Justin's brother doesn't know you're here."

"It's OK," Justin said quickly.

Like a good chauffeur, Robbie got out of the car quickly and moved over to the side door. He carried a phone book. Tugging on the door handle, he knocked sharply, his muffled voice coming through the window glass. "Who locked this?"

His eyebrows went up when three—not two—kids emerged.

"This is Tony, Gina's brother," Justin said. "We rescued him from a street gang."

Tony shook his head. "It wasn't a street gang," he said apologetically. "Just some kids."

"Well, nice to meet you," Robbie said. "Come along and join us for lunch."

"Thanks," Tony said gratefully, and they went inside. Soon the four of them had filled white bowls with noodles and all kinds of vegetables and had handed them to the grill chefs.

As Justin stood with the others watching their food sizzle, he looked more closely at Tony. *I wonder why he's wearing an Israeli Defense Force T-shirt,* Justin thought. *His last name's Coggins, and that doesn't sound Jewish.*

Above the sound of the sizzling grill they could hear the *Bomber* overhead.

Robbie grinned and glanced at the brother and sister. "Your dad seems like he's having fun up there."

"He is," Gina agreed.

"Justin," Tony said excitedly, "you've really gotta go up in the *Bomber*. Flying upside down is great!"

"That's OK," Justin responded faintly.

"Well, you'd better get used to flying, because when the rapture hits, *whoosh*—up you're gonna go," Tony commented.

Robbie eyed Tony curiously, and Justin said nothing.

When they got their platters of food, with brown rice on the side, Robbie led them over to a couple of booths by the window. "You guys sit in this one," he said. "I'll take the next one over so I can study the phone book and map my afternoon's route." He set his platter on the table in the next booth and was soon flipping pages.

Gina looked alarmed, and whispered to Justin, "We don't have to stay with Robbie all day, do we?"

"Let's take a bus home," Tony suggested. "I need to stop at Prof. McAndry's house."

"You must like that lighthouse a lot," Justin said. "To skip camp for it, I mean."

Tony grinned. "Yeah, it's really cool. Prof. McAndry gave me my own little room in the tower."

Justin stared. "You've got your own room? In the lighthouse?"

Gina spoke up. "Tony spent almost every day out there this summer pulling weeds, picking up trash, and planting flowers. I guess Prof. McAndry thought that if he's spending so much time out there, why not let him use a room?"

Tony nodded. "It's not really a room—just kind of a large closet. But it has its own little round window and an electric socket for power. I've got a lot of my stuff out there. And I can padlock it on the outside or the inside, to keep the Spooks out."

Justin's fork, holding a mix of noodles and veggies, paused halfway to his mouth. "Uh, you've got ghosts in the lighthouse?"

"No, the Spooks. It's a gang."

Justin's eyebrows came together, puzzled. "You mean those kids who chased you?"

Gina shook her head. "Not them. The Spooks are real burglars. Our town has had a lot of house robberies over the past several months. You go to bed at night, and you wake up in the morning and your computer's gone, your TV's gone, your antiques are gone. Nobody hears anything. That's why everybody calls them the Spooks."

"I've got a bunch of newspaper clippings about them filed in the back of my prayer notebook out at the lighthouse," Tony said.

Gina munched a delicious snow pea pod. "Tony's the notebook man."

"Not really," Tony said. "I'm just on this prayer Web site where we pray for people who aren't ready for the rapture. It's a pretty good site, and it's gotten a whole lot more exciting, especially in the last year. Pastor Dave is even trying to get some of the *Left Behind* books uploaded to the site."

They ate in silence for a while, enjoying the flavor of the food. Finally Robbie closed the phone book and glanced over at the others. "You guys about ready to go?"

Justin quickly gulped his final three bites, and he and his two new friends got to their feet. "Robbie," he said, "Gina and Tony know how to get home on the bus. Can I go with them?"

"It's not too far," Gina said.

Robbie paused for a moment, trying to think of any possible dangers. "OK," he finally said. "But leave a message for me at the dorm when you get back to the Cogginses' so I'll know you're all right."

"OK," Justin promised.

On the metro bus Tony sat next to Justin. After they'd ridden a couple of blocks, Tony reached into his back pocket, pulled out a stack of little pamphlets, and selected one. "You're saved, right?" he asked. "Now we need to get you to the next level."

"Tony, back off," Gina said in exasperation.

"Get thee behind me, persecutor," he said over his shoulder to Gina. Turning back to Justin, Tony tapped his wristwatch and said solemnly, "In 30 seconds I might vanish."

Justin looked startled. "Somebody's after you?" he asked. "Is it those kids on the street?"

"No, the rapture."

"By the way, Tony," said Gina, "why were those kids chasing you?"

"They were *persecuting* me," he corrected her. "I was telling one of them about the rapture."

"How old was your victim this time?" Gina asked.

Tony rolled his eyes at Gina's sarcasm, then

said, "I was informing a naive 9-year-old."

"Well, see?" she sputtered. "You're 12. You were picking on him, and the other kids didn't like it. And I don't blame them."

"Gina," said Tony in a level voice, "what if the rapture happened 30 seconds from now?"

"What's the rapture?" Justin asked.

"Oh, no, Justin!" Gina moaned. "Don't ask him that. He'll keep you trapped for three hours telling you about it."

"I thought you said you were saved," Tony said to Justin. "If you're really saved, you should already know about the rapture."

Justin was confused.

"Anyway, here, take this." Tony offered a little pamphlet to Justin. The title on the cover was in large blue letters: "What to Do if You Miss the Rapture."

"The rapture," Tony explained, "is Jesus' coming in the sky. When He does, all the born-again people will vanish."

Justin blinked. "Vanish?"

"Yes, vanish," Tony insisted. He pushed the pamphlet into Justin's hand. "Read this, and you'll understand why I tell people about it. Because if you're saved, you'll vanish with all the other born-again people, and you'll go to heaven to be with Jesus. But if you're not, you'll be stuck down here for another seven years, and you'll have to go through a horrible time called the tribulation with the rest of the unsaved people."

"Just a minute," said Justin. "I thought that when Jesus came—"

"Here's the college," Gina interrupted. She reached up and pulled a cord above the window, and a bell bonged. The bus stopped at the next corner, and the three young people got off in front of a large brick gateway.

Port Bradley College was partly old and partly new. Around the outside edges of the campus stood tall buildings with lots of glass—a sports arena, a science building, and a couple of large dorms. But in the center were three smaller granite buildings with square towers, which looked more than 100 years old.

"I'll take Justin home," Gina said to her brother. "You can go to Prof. McAndry's house."

"No, come along with me," her brother urged. "I want Justin to meet Prof. McAndry." He looked at Justin. "She's not saved, and this way when you pray for her you'll be able to picture her in your mind."

Justin nodded slowly, uneasily.

When they'd walked past the main part of campus, the group came to several little houses made of the same kind of granite used in the college buildings. Tony led the way as he turned in at the sidewalk of the fourth house.

They climbed its front steps, and Tony rang the doorbell.

"Prof. McAndry's been teaching history here at PBC for 20 years," he said while they waited. "But the lighthouse is her hobby."

"More like her *passion,"* Gina corrected him.

"Yeah," Tony agreed. "Her grandfather was rescued from a shipwreck in an ocean liner called the S.S. *Republic*. There was a huge storm, and the only thing that kept the ship from getting into deeper trouble was the gleam from the lighthouse."

He pressed the doorbell a couple more times, but got no response. "Let's go try at the back door," he said, leading the way around the house. "Sometimes she's in her bedroom watching the History Channel. One time she let me watch a documentary about when modern Israel became a nation in 1948. "

But the minute he'd raised his knuckles to the old wood panels of the rear door he stopped. "Oh, brother!" he moaned. "I forgot! She's out at the lighthouse today; probably spent last night there too, getting ready for the dedication. I was supposed to meet her there this afternoon. Getting chased and jumping into your limo made me forget!"

As Tony turned away, Justin paused and gave a close look at the door.

“She didn’t shut her door all the way,” he said. “There’s a little gap.”

Tony glanced at it and chuckled. “It’s an old house and an old door. It probably just *looks* loose.” He put his palm against the wood and pushed hard. The door swung inward and slammed against the wall. *“Whoa.”*

Justin pointed. “Tony. Gina. Look.”

Together they stared at the badly splintered doorframe.

Tony’s jaw fell. “Did I do that?”

Justin shook his head. “Crowbar, probably. Somebody’s broken in.”

Three

Looks Like Spooks

"Oh, great." Tony's voice sounded numb and foggy. "Oh, *great.* I wonder what they took." He stepped toward the doorway.

"Stop!" Gina and Justin called at the same instant.

But Tony kept going. Gina reached out, grabbed him by his belt, and hauled him back. "Tony! Remember what Dad said."

"Right," Justin whispered. "My dad told me the same thing. Never enter a house that looks like it's been broken into. The burglars might still be in there."

"But this has the Spooks written all over it," Tony objected. "They're long gone."

"Let's call the police," Gina said. "Where's the nearest phone?"

Tony shook off his sister's gripping hand. "That building," he said in a low voice, pointing to one of the granite structures. "You go call, and Justin and I will keep watch."

"We'll wait over in those trees," Justin said, and Tony grudgingly agreed. "And remember to tell them that the burglar may still be here. That should get them over here faster." The two boys ran toward a clump of trees a half block away, and Gina dashed toward the granite building.

No more than five minutes later a police car arrived, lights flashing but with no sirens. Gina still hadn't returned, which meant she was probably on the phone to her mom. Two police officers emerged from the car. One cautiously entered the house while the other closely studied the doorframe.

"Look," Tony said, "they're not even drawing their guns. They think it's the Spooks too."

The two boys left their hiding place and jogged toward the house. "Sir," Tony said to the police officer, who was now taking photographs of the splintered doorframe, "I'm Tony Coggins. I'm a friend of Prof. McAndry's. I'm helping her with the lighthouse renovation."

"Coggins?" The police officer, who had gray hair, looked him over from head to foot. "Are you Austin Coggins' boy?"

"Yes, sir."

"You look like him. Do you know where the owner is?"

"Prof. McAndry's probably out at the lighthouse."

The police officer sighed. "No phone out there, I'll bet. Does he have a mobile?"

Tony grinned. "Prof. McAndry is a woman. Yeah, she's got one, but she's always letting it go dead. My friend and I will probably have to go out there and tell her. She's got a little powerboat, and she'll get back right away."

The officer's frown turned to a look of frustration. "We're short on help right now," he said. "Tell your dad to quit his computer teaching job and get back on the force where he belongs." He glanced at his watch. "So you wouldn't mind going out to the lighthouse right now?"

"Could I go inside first and see what's missing?"

The police officer seemed about to say no, but then shouted, "Mike! All clear?"

"Clear," said a muffled voice from inside.

"Two kids coming in, friends of the owner. Might be able to give us a first lead on what's been taken." The police officer gestured toward the door. "Since you're Coggins' boy, you probably know not to touch anything. You too, son," he said to Justin. "Hands in your pockets the whole time."

Justin had never seen the inside of a history professor's house. But from the first glance at Prof. McAndry's home he could tell what her real interest was. Lighthouse paintings lined the walls. Little ceramic and wooden and stone lighthouses stood in every glass case and on top of every mantel. A lighthouse-shaped clock ticked on the wall, and rugs woven with lighthouse scenes crisscrossed the floor. Even the lamps on the tables were lighthouses.

He poked Tony in the ribs. "I wonder what this woman's hobby is," he said.

Tony chuckled. "Actually, most of these lighthouses are gifts from students. A lot of the students come from overseas, and once they get back home they hunt around for little lighthouses and send them to Prof. McAndry. Every week or so she gets a new package."

Tony led Justin swiftly from room to room, snarling as he discovered each new theft. Mike, the other officer, followed them with a notebook. "TV's gone," Tony growled. "VCR. DVD player. *No!*" he shouted.

"What's wrong?" the officer asked.

"The *Republic's* gone too!" Tony wailed. "It was this huge model of the ship Prof. McAndry's grandfather was rescued from. It's really valuable. It's like three feet long and has genuine gold fittings, an ebony hull and smokestacks, and an ivory deck."

Officer Mike wrote busily. He asked Tony what he could remember about makes and models of the other missing items and then asked, "Anything else?"

Glumly Tony looked around some more. "The

computer's gone," he said. "It was an older-model Compaq. She didn't use it a lot." He sighed. "That's the big stuff, anyway."

"Thanks," said Officer Mike. "We'll have to confirm all of this with Prof. McAndry, but at least now we can send an early e-mail to the pawnshops."

"Does it look like the Spooks?"

"Possibly," the police officer said cautiously.

Outside, the boys spotted Gina walking toward them from the building where she'd made the phone call. They joined her, and all three hurried across campus.

"Sorry I'm so late," she said. "I called Mom, and she told me to call Dad on his cell phone, and then college security. They'll keep an eye on her house until she gets back."

"The police think it may have been the Spooks," Tony said. "And they got the *Republic.*"

Gina's jaw dropped. "No way!"

Tony nodded.

"Oh, no!" Gina wailed. "Her grandpa spent years making it out of really expensive materials," she explained to Justin.

"We've got to get out to the lighthouse," Tony said.

They dropped by Robbie's dorm room, and while Justin dashed off a quick note to his brother, Tony tried to reach the professor on her cell phone.

"Dead again, like I thought," he said. "Let's go."

They jogged the three blocks to the water, and began stumbling along over the sand and rocks on a narrow, mile-long spit of land curving out toward a distant lighthouse, which gleamed white against the blue sky. Every few seconds they saw a tiny bright blink from its tower.

"It looks awesome," Justin said.

Tony nodded. "The painters did a great job. After Prof. McAndry's grandfather retired, he was a volunteer lighthouse keeper for part of each year. He did a lot of work on it, but after he died nobody else kept it up. Prof. McAndry has been working for years to restore it, and finally the dedication's going to happen this Sunday." His face fell, and he glared blackly at the sky. "Sometimes I wonder," he growled.

"About what?" asked Justin.

"About God and how He handles things." Tony kicked savagely at a jagged gray stone about the size of a golf ball.

"God didn't steal the *Republic,*" Gina said.

"Yeah, but why didn't He protect it? I've been praying for Prof. McAndry for a year! Now she's gonna think God doesn't really care."

"Tony, I think you'd better start minding your own business."

"Gina, there's no time *left* to mind my own

business! The Bible says the rapture is going to happen any time now!"

Gina rolled her eyes.

"Actually, I have a question," Justin said mildly as they trudged along. "It's about this 'rapture.' What exactly is it again?"

Tony glanced curiously at him. "I just can't believe it. You're a Christian and you've never heard that Jesus is coming back?"

"I've heard about His second coming," Justin replied, "but not about how everybody's going to vanish when it happens."

Tony thought a minute. "You know," he finally said, "I think the best thing would be for you to read that little rapture pamphlet I gave you, and then see if you have any questions."

"Whew," Gina said. "Saved from a Bible lecture!"

But Tony said softly, "Maybe God is warning Prof. McAndry about the end-times." He scuffed his foot in the sand. "Maybe He's showing her that we shouldn't value our possessions too much."

Justin glanced at Gina, who simply shook her head.

Four

Welcome to Headquarters

Justin had expected the history professor to be short and stocky. She wasn't. Even though her blond hair had gray streaks in it, Prof. McAndry was tall and thin, and looked like British royalty. She was painting the wood trim around the lighthouse door when her three visitors arrived. There was a smear of green paint on the edge of her left ear.

"Hi, Tony. Hi, Gina," she said cheerfully. "Who's your friend?"

After Justin had been introduced, Prof. McAndry swept an elegant hand toward the lighthouse. "What do you think of the trim?" she asked them. "Doesn't dark green go nicely with white? I'm so glad the painter was able to do not only the lighthouse but the shed and the keeper's house, too."

"Prof. McAndry," Tony said solemnly, "we've got some bad news for you."

Openmouthed, she listened to his story. Her face twisted in pain when she heard about the *Republic*. "That's the worst part," she said in a low voice. "I can replace the TV and the computer and everything else, but the *Republic* is one of a kind." She blinked rapidly to keep away the tears, then glanced around.

"Tony," she sighed, "can you help me lock up? You have your keys with you, don't you? Just pop the lid back on the paint can and rinse out the brush. You know where they go. Thanks. I'm sorry I don't have more life jackets out here for you all, or I'd take you back in the boat—it's faster than walking. But I really appreciate your tromping all the way out here to tell me."

"That's OK, Prof. McAndry," Tony said. "Anyway, I want to show Justin my room."

Grabbing a black leather fanny pack from the grass next to the lighthouse, the professor ran down to where a small gray motorboat was tied to a post next to the water. Soon she was sputtering away toward the mainland, leaving the three kids looking sadly after her.

"I wish there was something we could do," Tony said.

"We could pray," Justin said.

"Good idea," said Tony quickly. "Who's first?"

And right there by the lighthouse, with the wind and the cry of seagulls in their ears, they prayed that the *Republic* would be found and the Spooks captured.

When they'd finished, Gina said, "All three of

us are police officers' kids. We ought to be able to think of something. Hey, wait a minute, Justin," she said, turning to stare at him. "Your brother told Mom last night about how you've solved a bunch of cases."

Justin gave a modest shrug. "Not a whole lot," he said.

"What do you mean, not a whole lot?" she protested. "There was that radio station in Belize, a stolen painting, and some sort of temple mystery in Arizona. And there was something about a crystal dragon. Didn't you go to Kenya, too?"

Justin blushed. "I had a lot of help," he said. "Dad's just always told me to keep my eyes open and notice things."

Tony nodded. "That's what our dad tells us to do."

"Well, then," his sister said, "why can't we figure this out, the three of us? Let's try. We shouldn't let the *Republic* disappear without fighting for it."

The other two agreed, and then Tony turned toward the lighthouse. "First, come and see my room," he said to Justin.

The lighthouse, with its gleaming white paint job, was actually just a little taller than a telephone pole. Its round tower thrust up from a corner of a little one-story building. At the tower's top was a balcony with a white metal railing, and behind it a curved glass window.

Justin followed Tony through the green door of the building into an open room with lots of maps on the wall. A large empty glass case stood on a wooden table.

"That," Gina said, "was where Prof. McAndry was going to display the *Republic.*"

Tony led them to a corner of the room, where a circular staircase with metal steps ascended into the tower. After one turn of the steps he stopped in front of a small door, which was locked with a huge padlock. Pulling a ring of keys from his pocket, he selected one and inserted it. There was an impressive click.

"This room," he said over his shoulder to Justin as he removed the padlock, "is big-time *secure.*"

He led the way inside, and Justin's jaw sagged in amazement. The curved wall of the tiny room was covered from floor to ceiling with photos, maps and charts. Most of the maps were of Israel, some with Hebrew lettering on them. There were several photos of Jerusalem from different directions and time line charts with different colored lines stretching from the past through the current year and into the future.

A large piece of cardboard had been covered with a circle and some clock numbers. Hand printing across the top of the clock said "Rapture Countdown" and two cardboard clock-hands had been attached, which stood exactly at 12:00.

In the center of all the wall displays was a dusty porthole window about the size of a dinner plate. Through it Justin could see blue sky and a little of the town in the distance. On the floor beside an army cot covered with a green blanket were several cardboard file boxes and some white plastic ones. An old laptop computer stood open on a small metal table, and beside its keyboard was a Bible, a small radio with an antenna, and a framed picture of a smiling young man holding an open Bible.

"Wow," Justin commented, wide-eyed. "This room is yours?"

"Prof. McAndry's letting me use it," Tony said. "And I can lock it from the inside, too." He closed the door and held up the padlock. "I'm totally safe." He swung a hasp shut and snapped the padlock, locking the threesome inside the room.

"Don't lose that key," Gina said nervously, "or break it."

"Don't worry," her brother said. He put the key ring back in his right jeans pocket and flicked on the little radio, which instantly started hissing. Every once in a while Justin could hear faint garbled words.

"Shortwave," Tony explained. "It's an English-speaking Israeli station."

"I noticed your shirt," Justin said. "And all these maps. Are you guys Jewish?"

Tony shook his head. "I just like to keep track of what Israel's doing," he said. "Especially the defense force."

Gina rolled her eyes. "He thinks it helps him know how close the rapture is," she said, clearly annoyed.

"One of these days you won't make fun of me," Tony snapped. Reaching into his left pocket, he removed the fat wad of paper and the floppy disk and placed them beside the laptop.

"Can you get on the Internet out here?" Justin asked.

Tony shook his head. "No phone line. I get on to Pastor Dave's Web site back home and do a hard copy printout and a diskette and store them here."

"Is that a picture of Pastor Dave?" Justin asked, pointing.

Tony nodded. "He was our youth pastor for a while. Now he's in England taking seminary training. For a while he thought he would close down his Web page, but he decided to keep it going after all. So he still keeps up the Web site from there."

"What's the site for?" Justin wanted to know.

"It gives the latest news about Israel and Bible prophecy, but it's mainly for prayer. Everybody sends in prayer requests, and we pray for them."

"My brother needs to get a life," Gina said to Justin.

Justin glanced at her. "There's nothing wrong with prayer, is there?"

"Yeah, Gina," said Tony. "And I'm not the only one doing it. A lot of kids send prayer requests to Pastor Dave's Web site, and we all pray."

"Sure, prayer is good," she agreed, "but why put so much technology into it?"

"Gina, don't talk like that!" Tony said heatedly. "Look, what if the rapture happened right now? What would happen to people like Uncle Louie and Prof. McAndry?"

Justin tactfully cleared his throat. "Uh, what's in those boxes there?"

"My files," Tony said.

"No, I mean those plastic ones."

Tony bent down and opened one, to reveal lots of plastic bags with pieces of bread in them. "Zwieback," he said.

"What's zwieback?"

"It's German for 'twice-baked.' You put pieces of whole-wheat bread in the oven and bake them with a slow heat. They end up crunchy, but once they're baked like that they won't spoil. Sort of like crackers."

Justin stared at the white boxes. "Is that all there is in there—zwieback?"

"Try a piece."

Justin took a piece and started chewing. "Needs ketchup."

Gina snickered.

"What's in those bottles?" Justin asked. "Water?"

"Yes, water," Gina interjected.

"I just want to be ready," Tony said. "I mean, if I don't make it, well, that means I'll be stuck here on earth for another seven years."

Gina's voice softened. "Jesus loves you, Tony."

He nodded several times. "I know. I know He does. But what if—"

"Get a life!" Gina said curtly. "You and your long prayer lists. You act as though you've got to save the whole world. Jesus did that already."

Tony just stared at her. Justin could see that his eyes were red-rimmed. Tony had either been losing sleep or was in the habit of crying a lot. And before they left, he grabbed a large three-ring notebook and carried it with him.

Five

THE MERRY-THON

"Aha, my victim has arrived!" shouted Austin Coggins as the three kids entered the living room.

If Justin had remembered that his father's former fellow police officer would be waiting to pounce, he would have headed to the dorm and come to the Cogginses' house after the man was in bed. But there was Mr. Coggins, big as life, watching TV and wearing an old leather pilot's helmet.

"Dad," Gina said in disgust, "that thing *stinks.*"

"No, it doesn't," her father said, taking the helmet off and sniffing at it. "That's the neat's-foot oil I rub on it to keep it soft. This is in perfect shape," he told Justin. "Barnstormers and wing walkers wore this kind of thing in the 1930s. So did Lindbergh on his way to Paris." The man rose to his feet and carried the helmet over to a tall glass case and carefully replaced it among several other old-time flying souvenirs—a sextant, a large compass, brown leather flying boots, goggles, and a water canteen. Then he fixed Justin with a meaningful gaze. "I wear that helmet every time I go up in the *Bomber,*" he said.

"Th-that's great," said Justin feebly.

"Tomorrow is going to be even sunnier than today," Mr. Coggins announced thoughtfully, stroking his beard. "Don't pass up the chance to let me strap you into my beautiful biplane."

"Not tomorrow, Dad," Tony said. "We're going to Uncle Pete's cabin for a picnic, remember? You said we could, since your classes don't start until next Monday. Justin, you come too, OK?"

Trying not to show his relief at another day of earthbound safety, Justin shook his head. "Sorry. I've got to document Robbie."

Mr. Coggins flicked a curious glance at him. "Document Robbie? What does that mean?"

"Frosh bash is tomorrow."

Mr. Coggins' eyes lit up. He chuckled. "Oh, boy. I forgot your brother was a freshman. Poor kid. I'll bet he has to wear the beanie. Do they still do the beanie?"

Justin nodded. "A little yellow and purple cap."

"And he's got to do the Merry-thon? The tricycles, the stilts, the canoes?"

Tony said, "Dad went to Port Bradley College too—a long, long time ago."

"Hey," his father growled, "not so long ago as that. So they're still doing frosh bash? Wow. Get to the freshmen early and intimidate them, I guess."

Tony sighed. "So you can't come with us, Justin?"

"Sorry," Justin said again. "I've got to go along and take pictures to prove that Robbie did everything he was supposed to do."

Mr. Coggins gave one wistful look across the room at the case containing his helmet and the other flying treasures, and then turned on Justin with a fierce frown. "You have escaped me theez once," he hissed in an excellent Dracula imitation, "but I weel be back! You weel fly in zee *Bomber* soon!"

Later, as Justin and Tony were getting ready for bed, Tony handed him the three-ring binder he'd carried back from the lighthouse. "Would you do something for me?" he asked.

"Sure," Justin said. "What?"

"Read this. It's all the news articles about the Spooks."

Justin said cautiously, "I don't think I'll be able to solve the cases just by reading about them."

Tony shook his head impatiently. "You don't have to solve them, just pray about them. Pray that somehow we'll find the *Republic* so Prof. McAndry will know that God is powerful." He placed the notebook in Justin's hands. "And I put some of my prayer lists in there too. You promise to pray?"

Justin nodded. "Sure."

* * *

Just as Mr. Coggins had predicted, the next day was sunny. As Justin stood with his brother at 8:00 a.m. in the college's large parking lot, he was glad that the Coggins family and their fanatical flying father were far away. *We need rain,* Justin thought, glancing moodily at the cheerful sky. *Lots of rain and low clouds every day until next week, when I go back home.*

"All right, who do we have here?" A stocky college student with glasses hurried up to them, carrying a clipboard.

Robbie sighed. "Robert Case, Jr.," he said.

Justin looked at his brother and once again tried to keep from laughing. They were standing beside a large adult-sized tricycle, and Robbie was wearing not only the little yellow-and-purple cap but also a yellow-and-purple athletic shirt with a picture of a bear on it, and yellow-and-purple athletic shorts. Over the shirt he wore a bright-orange life vest. All around them in the parking lot were a lot of other freshmen in yellow and purple and orange, some with trikes, some with canoes, and some trying to climb up on stilts.

"Beanie, shirt, shorts," said the student, checking off boxes on the clipboard paper. "What's the special cry?"

Robbie closed his eyes and took a breath.

"Go, Bears, go. Go, Bears, go. Go-giddy-go-giddy-go-go-go."

"Howl it," said the student firmly. "Like a bear."

Robbie glanced at him doubtfully. "Do bears howl?"

The student frowned. "Port Bradley College Bears howl. Howl it!"

"Go, Bears, go!" howled Robbie. "Go, Bears, go! Go-giddy-go-giddy-go-go-go!"

"That's better," said the student, making a mark on his clipboard. Justin kept his mouth very straight and serious, but the muscle strain was awful.

"And when do you utter the special cry?" the student quizzed.

"When anybody asks me to," replied Robbie.

"All right, then. Get on your trike and get in line." The student suddenly glanced at Justin. "Wait. Who's this?"

"My brother," Robbie said. "He's going to document me."

The student looked doubtful. "Well, OK," he finally said. "But remember, he rides with you. Everywhere."

"On the trike too?" Robbie asked. "There's no room."

"On the trike too," the student said. "If you bring a documenter, he's got to ride with you on everything. And he has to be on stilts, too. Not yours, but another pair." He hurried off to greet another arriving freshman.

Robbie sighed and mounted the trike, and Justin began experimenting with various footholds on the back. None worked.

"Then get on the handlebars," Robbie growled. "But not until we start."

A few minutes later a girl student spoke through a bullhorn and welcomed the large group of freshmen to the campus. After trying unsuccessfully to teach them the school song, she read out some complicated Merry-thon rules and then shouted, "Go!"

Justin jumped up and sat on the handlebars, and dozens of trikes began to trundle forward. Off to the side the canoe carriers headed toward the water, and from every direction there arose a nervous clattering of stilts.

"Justin, your backpack is in my face," Robbie said sternly. "Get it off. I'll put it in the basket behind my seat. Whoa!" he said as he transferred it. "This weighs a ton. What's in here?"

"Your camera," Justin said sympathetically, "and a notebook Tony gave me. And our water bottles."

"I wish this trike had more than one gear," Robbie grumbled, pedaling as fast as he could.

The idea of the Merry-thon was to ride on one method of transportation to a certain point, then switch to another method, and then to a third. There didn't seem a whole lot of pressure to win, just to complete the three trips and to always be ready to utter the "Go, Bears, go!" cry if someone requested it.

The only other hassle was the townspeople, who loved the Merry-thon because it gave them a chance to poke some good-natured fun at the college kids. They would call out from their front yards or roll down their car windows if they were driving by. "What's that special cry again?" they would shout and each time Robbie had to launch hoarsely into "Go, Bears, go."

"I'm going to be glad for two things," he moaned after they'd gone several blocks. "The first is for this morning to be over, and the second is getting to be a sophomore so I can harass the next crop of freshmen."

Guess what? Justin thought to himself. *I am going to get really bored today. I wish I'd never said yes to Robbie.* "We're on Brevard Street," he announced, glancing at a street sign ahead and then at a little map in his hand. "Turn right here, at Meridian. Only eight more blocks to go."

"What do you mean, *only* eight more blocks?" Robbie snorted, steering around a tan repair van with the sign "Coffman Plumbing" on the side and some ladders on top. "Take a picture," he said suddenly, slowing to a stop. "They want a picture of me on the trike, the stilts, and the canoe. We forgot to take it at the parking lot. Remind me to get this roll developed at Wal-Mart tonight. I'll sure be glad when I can afford a digital camera," he added.

Justin jumped off the handlebars, grabbed the backpack from the basket, and ran a few yards ahead, fumbling in the backpack for the camera. He aimed it back at Robbie and snapped the shot.

"Robbie," he said once he was balanced on the handlebars again, "what do you know about the rapture?"

"I've heard of it, but I don't know very much about it," he panted. "Why do you want to know?"

"Tony believes in something called the rapture. He thinks that when Jesus comes, the righteous people are just going to vanish." He told his brother about Tony and his booklets and his Israeli Army T-shirt and his lighthouse room and the boy's worries. "Gina thinks that it's getting Tony a little unbalanced," Justin finished.

"You think he's dangerous?" Robbie asked.

"Nah, I don't think so." Justin paused a minute to wonder. "It's just that Tony gets himself upset thinking about how a lot of people won't be ready for the rapture. Sometimes he worries that *he* won't be either."

"That's kinda sad." Robbie shifted himself on

the seat and peered around his brother's side. "How many more blocks?"

"Six."

"You sure it's not four?"

Justin took a little paper map out of his shirt pocket and peered at it. "Six. Cranshaw, Park Lane, Augustine, Maple Drive, Oak Drive, and then Beech Drive."

"Is this kid a Christian?" Robbie asked.

"Yeah."

"Then how come he's so worried about Jesus' return?"

"Like I said, he hopes he's ready but he's not sure. And he thinks that if he misses the rapture he'll have to survive for seven more years down here. He's got tons of water and dried bread in the lighthouse, just in case."

"The kid sounds like he's got a screw loose."

"No," Justin said, "he's just really worried. And he's even more upset because the Spooks stole Prof. McAndry's model ship." Justin told his brother about the theft and how they'd gone all the way out to the lighthouse to tell the professor about it.

"Hey," Robbie said sharply, panting with alarm, "don't get mixed up in another one of your adventures. Dad's too far away to bail you out, and I don't have the time. I'm supposed to keep you safe until you fly out again next

Tuesday. So try to make it easy for me, OK?"

Justin shrugged. "I'm not looking for trouble."

"Well, if you see it coming, dodge it." Robbie steered the trike over to the curb. "Let's rest," he said wearily. "And one of these days you're going to have to go on a diet. What have you been eating, anyway?"

After Robbie had dismounted the trike he did some stretching exercises. "You watch out, Justin," he said warningly. "These Spooks, whoever they are, have the whole campus scared. This morning before the Merry-thon started the dean got the whole dorm together and told us to keep our rooms locked when we weren't in them. I guess the Spooks are so good that the police are always six or seven steps behind them."

"Can you get on the Internet in the dorm?" Justin asked.

Robbie bent down and touched his toes, groaning. "Yeah, why?"

"I want to download some facts about the rapture, but I want to do it someplace besides the Cogginses' house."

"I guess we could do it at noon, after this Merry-thon stuff is done with," Robbie said. "You could print out some stuff, and we could talk it over this afternoon in the limo."

"Thanks."

Finally Robbie pedaled painfully into the

Beech Drive parking lot, where another freshman was waiting to take over the trike, and he and Justin got their stilts. Thankfully, their dad had made them stilts when they were younger, so after Justin had snapped Robbie's picture they had no problem clunking the five blocks to a parking lot near the water where several canoes, gleaming wet, waited for them.

"Life jacket," a student said to Robbie when they got there.

"I'm wearing it," Robbie said, annoyed and thumping his chest.

"I mean for your documenter," said the student.

"Oh, no," Robbie moaned. "I never thought of him."

Try as they might, they couldn't find a spare vest for Justin.

"Guess you'll have to paddle by yourself then, Case," the student said. "Documenter, you wait right here. Nobody goes in a canoe without a life jacket."

So Justin sat on a park bench under a covered shelter watching Robbie paddle earnestly away in his canoe. This was the hardest event of the Merry-thon; freshmen were supposed to canoe halfway out to the lighthouse and back. Powerboats buzzed back and forth to make sure they completed the whole route and to rescue anyone if a canoe tipped over.

Well, Justin thought to himself, *here's my chance to look through Tony's notebook.* And by the time Robbie returned and staggered over to the park bench, Justin had gone through the entire notebook several times. He'd read through the Spooks newspaper clippings, through lots of information about Israel, and through prayer requests such as "Please pray for Hector, who has hepatitis C and is in the hospital" and "Jesus is coming soon; pray for Betty, Marvin, Cassandra, and Leslie and their music ministry" and "Lord, help my bike get through the school year without breaking."

"Let's get out of here," Robbie groaned. "If there is such a thing as the rapture, I need it to happen right now."

In Robbie's dorm room Justin spent 20 minutes online downloading several different opinions about the rapture. While he printed these out, Robbie changed into his limo driver's uniform. "Ready?" the older brother said. "What do you say we go to the Mongolian Grill again?"

"Yeah!" Justin yelped. "I've got a little money. I can pay for mine."

"No, you earned your meal by being my documenter," Robbie said, "and I earned mine by hauling you around on my handlebars." He shuddered. "Well, at least we don't have to go through *that* again."

First they dropped Robbie's film roll off for one-hour processing at Wal-Mart, and then they went to the Mongolian Grill. After a delicious, relaxing meal (this time there was no *Bomber* buzzing overhead), Justin and Robbie rode together for several hours, talking about Jesus' second coming and people's different opinions about it and what they understood the Bible to really say about it.

Whenever Robbie stopped to deliver a business card, Justin got out and looked into the windows of stores. Once they went to a huge mall and got waffle ice-cream cones. And finally, late in the afternoon, they picked up their developed pictures, put them in Justin's backpack, and went back to Robbie's dorm. Justin watched CNN in the lobby until he thought the Cogginses might be back, then went to a phone booth near the door and dialed their number.

"Hello?" It was a woman's voice. She sounded as though she had a bad cold.

"Mrs. Coggins?" Justin asked cautiously. *If this is a wrong number, I'm in trouble,* he said to himself. *I don't have any more coins.*

"Oh, hello, Justin," the woman said. She didn't have a cold. Rather, she'd been crying.

"Mrs. Coggins, is something wrong?"

"No," she said. "I mean, yes. *Yes*. We've been robbed!"

Six

Spooked Again

Justin dashed up to Robbie's room to tell him the news and then raced across campus and down the street to the Cogginses' house. Gina stood in the driveway next to their two cars—a green Toyota along with the SUV they'd taken to the cabin that day. The girl's eyes were very large. She wore latex surgical gloves, and gave a pair to Justin.

"Put these on," she said, "so we don't spread any more fingerprints. And stay out of Dad's way. He is very, very angry. His pilot stuff is all gone."

Justin's jaw dropped. "Those things in the living room cabinet? His special helmet?"

"The helmet and everything else."

"Where's Tony?" he asked.

"Up in his room," she said. "Justin, I think he's crying. They got the computer, so now he can't keep in touch with his prayer Web site."

"And now's the time he needs it most," Justin said softly, tugging on the latex gloves. "Do you think it was the Spooks?"

"Of course it was the Spooks," the girl said

angrily. "They popped the back door the way they did at Prof. McAndry's house and just strolled in and took what they wanted. And all this time we were up at Uncle Pete's cabin having a picnic and not suspecting a thing."

"Did they get anything of yours?"

"Grandma's doll collection," she said in a quavery voice. "Just four dolls, that's all, but they were special. Grandma had made the clothes for them when she was a little girl."

As Justin followed Gina inside, his amateur detective skills automatically kicked in. He looked at the SUV, the Toyota, the driveway, the house, and the yard. "Keep your eyes open," his dad had always told him. "Don't miss a thing. Use as much of each retina as you can."

In the living room Austin Coggins was kneeling in front of the display cabinet. A black police briefcase was open on the floor beside him, and he was carefully brushing fingerprint powder on the wood and the glass. He'd moved the floor lamp very close so that the light shone brightly on the empty shelves.

"Justin," he commanded in a tight voice, "sit down. Right on the floor, right where you are. Unless you have to go to the bathroom," he added.

"No, I'm fine."

"Then stay there. I just want to make sure we've collected everything they might have dropped, every bit of fabric, whatever."

"Did you call the police?" Justin asked.

Mr. Coggins nodded. "I called them but told them I could handle it. They're short-staffed as it is, and the dispatcher told me that the Spooks hit another house a few blocks up."

Justin felt a tingle of fear along his back. "Two in a day?"

"These guys are very good at what they do." Mr. Coggins cleared his throat. "Now, I'm busy, so just stay still. Or go up and see Tony. Somebody needs to be with that poor kid. I'd do it if I wasn't doing this."

"Shall I take my shoes off?" Justin asked.

"No, leave them on. Socks will pick up things shoe heels can't. Just step lightly and don't scuff the carpet."

Justin's eyes traveled around the room. The big-screen TV was still there, but the DVD player was gone. He carefully moved across the room and went upstairs.

Tony was seated on the edge of his bed snapping the right cuff of his latex glove against his wrist, over and over. He looked thinner and paler than ever. Beside him on the covers was a shoe box with the lid off. Inside were lots of floppy disks.

"Tony," Justin said in a hushed voice, and then he didn't say anything else, because even if he'd known what to say he wouldn't have known how to say it.

Tony sighed. "Well, at least they didn't get my floppies. And I don't store anything on the hard drive anyway. It's all here"—he tapped the shoe box—"and copies are at the lighthouse. But now I don't have any way of getting to Pastor Dave's Web site. Unless I can get Dad to bring his laptop home from his office at the college."

"You can probably use Robbie's computer in the dorm."

His eyes lit up. "He'd let me do that?"

"I'm pretty sure he would," Justin assured him. "If you're just getting on and printing some things off and wouldn't do it during his study time, no problem."

"That'd be great. Thanks."

"What else did they take?"

Tony made a grinding sound with his teeth. "Gina's dolls, all Dad's pilot stuff, anything looking like an antique." He glared at the top of his dresser. "And they got my Israeli Army bush hat, too. I would have taken it to the cabin with me, but Gina teases me about it." He stared at Justin with his usual red-rimmed eyes. "Who *are* they, anyway? And why can't anybody stop them?"

"It's pretty daring, to come in here during the daytime."

Tony shuddered. "I guess they must have

been watching us or something. Somebody saw our whole family get in the SUV with a cooler and a picnic basket and take off and figured we'd be gone all day." He paused and gave Justin a funny look. "Did *you* tell anybody we were going to be gone?"

Justin shook his head.

"Neither did we," Tony said. "Dad always makes sure not to tell anybody our plans." He sighed. "But the Spooks got us anyway."

Gina appeared in the doorway, her face pale.

"Come in here, Gina," her brother said. "We've got to do *something.*"

She scowled. "Well, *that's* a change. I thought you were just going to sit there and babble, 'Well, this is the end-time, the rapture's gonna happen any minute now, nothin' we can do, so *there.*'"

"Do you have a sister, Justin?" Tony asked in a calm, deadly voice.

Justin shook his head.

"You don't know how lucky you are."

Gina leaned over the bed and tipped the floppy disks out of the shoe box, then darted back as Tony lunged at her.

"I've got an idea," Justin said hastily.

They turned to frown at him. "What about?" Tony asked.

"You mentioned we need to do something,"

Justin reminded him. "I've got an idea about what we can do."

"What?" Gina asked.

"Go on patrol."

Brother and sister stared at him stonily.

"I mean just sort of walk up and down the streets and keep our eyes open," Justin said. "The Spooks aren't invisible. They're real people who go into houses and carry things out of them. They're out there somewhere, and maybe we can spot them."

Gina sighed. "I apologize, Justin," she said. "We're both being kind of snotty." She took a trembly breath. "It's just—it's just really cruel for people to come into your house and steal whatever they want. I don't care," she said angrily to Tony, "if it *is* the last days. It's just really mean to come and take people's stuff away from them."

Tony nodded. "It sure is. Sorry, Gina. I didn't mean to make you feel worse." He glanced at Justin. "I guess we could try it. Your patrol idea, I mean. Tomorrow morning? Let's do it. And we won't walk—we'll go on bikes."

Seven

Sleuths on Patrol

"So what exactly are we looking for?" Gina asked the next morning after they'd put on their bike helmets. Mrs. Coggins lent her helmet to Justin, which to his dismay was a bright neon pink.

"We look for maid service cars," Tony said promptly. "In people's driveways."

Gina frowned. "You mean where two or three women go around in a station wagon and clean people's houses? What good is that going to do?"

"They've got keys to the houses. They could just walk in and get the stuff."

"Wait a minute," she said. "They've only got keys to their clients' houses, not everybody's."

"True," Justin agreed. "And if somebody with a maid service gets robbed, the maid service company would be the first one the police would check out."

"Besides," Gina said, "Prof. McAndry doesn't use a maid service, and neither do we."

"Another thing," Justin continued. "A maid's station wagon isn't big enough for the maids plus all the stuff they took from Prof. McAndry's house."

Gina nodded. "Yeah. It would look pretty weird for a maid service car to be driving down the street with TVs and computers and a doll collection in the back."

"OK, OK," Tony said. "Let's just look for *any* service vehicle parked in anybody's driveway. Moving vans, anything like that. If it looks strange, we take down the house's address and also the vehicle's license number."

"I brought a notebook," Justin said, slapping his back pocket.

"And let's make sure we act like kids," Gina reminded them, "not detectives."

Justin agreed. "If we see something suspicious, we ride on past. When we're out of sight, we stop and compare notes."

So for almost three hours they rode through town, acting like kids, doing wheelies, showing off to each other, jumping curbs—and keeping watch.

One time they saw a large gray truck backed up in someone's driveway. Around the corner of the next block they screeched to a stop.

"Tell me what you saw," Justin said, getting out his notebook. "License number?"

"Z46223H," Tony recited. "Chevy truck, I think."

Justin wrote this down, and said, "Gina, see anything interesting?"

She grinned. "Yeah. The back left tire was flat."

"No, it wasn't," Tony sputtered.

"Yes, it was," she insisted. "Want to go back and look? And there are lots of leaves and tree needles right around the tire. That truck hasn't gone anywhere for weeks." Her grin widened. "Remember, I'm a police officer's kid too."

Other than the gray truck, they didn't see anything unusual. Backhoes clawed at pavement, replacing sewer pipe. Cable company trucks lifted hard-hatted workers to the tops of telephone poles. Garbage trucks emptied big gray waste containers. But nothing unusual was parked in anyone's driveway, and nobody was carrying TVs or computers or precious family heirlooms out to waiting vehicles.

The kids took a break around noon to go to the food court in the nearby mall. As they shared a large pizza at a corner table, they talked together in low voices.

"Look, we were only out there for three hours," Gina pointed out. "It's the first half of just one day. The Spooks are going to be out stealing things *sometime* this week. Maybe it just wasn't this morning."

Justin chewed thoughtfully. "We're doing this wrong," he said.

"Why?" Tony wanted to know.

"The Spooks know things about people."

"That's what I've been telling you," Tony said

before he bit into his next pizza slice. "Somebody's watching houses, the way they watched ours. They see a whole family take off with a lot of stuff to go somewhere. They know the family's going to be gone for several hours."

Justin got a discontented look on his face. "That might be it," he said. "But—"

Gina interrupted him. "So what we have to look for this afternoon isn't strange vehicles in driveways, but people watching houses."

"Wait a minute," Justin replied. "Did we see anybody watching houses this morning?"

The other two had to confess that they hadn't.

"But we weren't *looking* for watchers," Tony reminded him. "I say let's ride around some more, and this time look for people just sitting in parked cars or watching from windows. And we'll take down their license numbers or their addresses."

The trio of sleuths got back on their bikes and headed onto the streets again for another hour. But again their search brought no results. The only people sitting in cars were in store parking lots—adults waiting for their spouses or kids to finish shopping. But out among the houses nobody sat in parked cars, and nobody sat staring out windows.

"This is totally useless," Tony finally said when they'd stopped at an intersection. "Let's go home."

"How do the Spooks *do* it?" Gina wailed. "We know they're out there. They're not imaginary."

"I've got another idea," Justin said.

The girl looked at him suspiciously. "If it means we have to ride our bikes all over town some more, forget it." She rubbed the top of her right leg just above her knee.

"Calm down, Gina," Tony said firmly. "If it's an idea that'll catch the Spooks and find the *Republic*—and your dolls—I'll get back on my bike and ride till midnight."

Gina sighed. "What's your idea, Justin?"

"We talk to people who got robbed."

"And ask them what?"

Justin shrugged. "Whether anybody knew they were going to be gone that day. Things like that."

"But some people weren't away," Tony replied.

"That's true," Gina said. "Sometimes the Spooks break in at night."

Justin shook his head. "Not in the newspaper clippings in your notebook, Tony. All the stories there say that the Spooks hit the houses when people were gone."

Gina frowned. "Are you sure?"

"I'm sure."

"Well, we could try talking to some of the people," said Tony, "starting with Prof. McAndry. But I'll bet we're not going to get very far."

"Why not?" Justin asked.

Tony spread out his hands, palms up. *"We* got robbed. Nobody knew we were going to be gone, unless they happened to see us leave." He pushed off with his bike. "But I guess we can try Prof. McAndry."

They found the tall, elegant history professor just leaving for the lighthouse.

"Prof. McAndry," Tony said, "may we ask you some questions about yesterday, when your house was robbed?"

She glanced at him curiously. "I suppose so."

Justin flashed her a charming, boyish grin. "We're amateur detectives," he said. "We want to see if we can solve the case and catch the Spooks."

"Oh, I see." Prof. McAndry was working hard to keep a straight face. "All right, go ahead and ask your questions."

Tony asked, "Did anybody know you were going to be gone yesterday?"

"Let's see." The professor paused while she thought. "Probably not," she finally said. "Classes don't start till next Monday, so I'm not tied to a schedule. Nobody needs to know when I come or go."

Gina said, "Of course, a lot of people know you're getting the lighthouse ready for the dedication ceremony on Sunday."

"How many people knew about the *Republic?"* Justin asked.

Prof. McAndry shut her eyes for a moment, and Justin could see worried lines around her weary eyes. “Most of the faculty did, I suppose,” she said. “I’ve had them over for parties. They’ve seen it.”

“Have the police found any of your things?” Gina inquired sympathetically.

The woman shook her head. “Nothing. Oh, by the way, do any of you know somebody who could fix a water leak?”

Gina and Tony looked at each other thoughtfully. “Not right offhand,” Gina said, “but I can ask Dad.”

“The water system in this old place has worked so well that I’ve never had to know any good plumbers,” Prof. McAndry continued. “But now the water line in the basement is leaking.”

“Wait,” Justin said. “Carlton Plumbing. No, *Coffman* Plumbing. I saw a truck of theirs yesterday while I was with my brother at the frosh bash.”

“I’ll give them a call,” Prof. McAndry said gratefully. “I put a bucket under the leak, so it should be all right for a while. Thank you. Oh, and I hope your car is feeling better.” She glanced at her watch and hurried away.

Gina glanced alertly at Tony, who was fishing for something in his pocket. “What did she just say?”

He blinked. "Prof. McAndry? She said she was going to call a plumber."

"No, after that."

He shrugged. "Guess I missed it."

"She said something about your car," Justin said.

Gina nodded. "Oh, yeah. Something about our car feeling better."

"Yeah, that was it," Tony replied.

"But our car hasn't been feeling sick," she said.

"The Toyota? Yes, it has," Tony said. "It's running rough. Dad says it needs a tune-up. He must've told her sometime recently." The boy finally found what he'd been looking for in his pocket: a smudged bit of paper. "Just a minute. I've gotta check on something."

From his backpack he took out a tiny radio and pulled its antenna out all the way. Clicking it on, he carefully turned the tuning knob, and the radio hissed and burbled.

"Shortwave," he explained. "I'll put my earphones on so it doesn't bother you."

"What's on shortwave?" Justin asked.

"BBC news. British Broadcasting Corporation. I get it through a Canadian station. It's not too clear in the daytime, but I get enough to understand what's going on. The BBC's got more news than U.S. radio does, and different kinds of news, too. There's more about the world."

"That's pretty cool," Justin said admiringly. "You must know a lot about the world by now."

Tony plugged the little earphone jack into the side of the radio, and the hissing stopped. "Not the whole world, just Israel."

"Why Israel?" Justin asked, even though from his rapture study he thought he knew.

"Didn't you read that booklet I gave you?" Tony demanded. "If you keep an eye on Israel, you'll know how close the rapture is." He held up his hand. "Now they're doing headlines. If Israel isn't in the headlines, I turn it off." He turned away from them, tilting and tipping the little radio for better reception.

"Can you believe my brother?" Gina remarked to Justin. "Normal kids skateboard. My brother listens to the BBC." She suddenly got an alert look on her face. "Justin, what was that you said about a plumbing truck?"

"You mean the one I saw yesterday?"

"Yes. You saw it parked in someone's driveway?"

He shook his head. "No, just along the street."

"Nobody was carrying anything toward it from a house?"

He grinned. "I thought of that, too. Not a sign of any Spooks. But I wrote 'Coffman Plumbing' in my notebook just in case."

"Hey, that's your name!" Gina said, laughing. "Justin Case. Get it?"

Justin blushed. "Yes, I'm quite aware of that fact."

"Well, anyway, I'm going to ask Dad to check out Coffman Plumbing," she stated.

"Two more bombings in Jerusalem," Tony reported with his back to them.

Gina rolled her eyes. "I almost wish he was old enough to get interested in girls," she whispered. "This Israel-rapture stuff just isn't healthy for him." The girl sighed. "Well, we're not getting very far with the Spook investigation. What do we do next?"

Justin shrugged. "We're at the Spooks' mercy," he said. "We just don't have enough to go on."

But two hours later the first break came.

Eight

Vandals' Visit

The break happened after Justin and the Coggins kids got home.

"Grab the newspaper, OK, Tony?" Gina said as they rode their bikes up the driveway.

Tony got out his house key, picked up the newspaper lying on the concrete, and opened the garage door from inside the house. When Gina and Justin had put away the bikes and joined him in the kitchen, he was carefully tearing a clipping from the paper.

"You still have my notebook, right?" he asked Justin.

Justin nodded. "But I left it in Robbie's dorm room. I can get it back to you tonight."

"Don't worry about it," Tony said. "Keep it as long as you want, if it'll help find the Spooks. Just put this with the rest of the clippings. It's the story about the two latest robberies, ours and the other one."

"Two in the same day." Justin took the clipping and scanned down it. "It says one of them happened on Acorn Street."

"That's us," Gina said.

Justin's eyes opened wider. "Look at this. The other robbery happened on Brevard. That's one of the streets Robbie and I drove down with the trike." He stared first at Tony, then at Gina. "I must have just missed it, unless it happened at some other time of the day."

"Did you see *anything* unusual?" Tony asked anxiously.

Justin thought back. "We got right onto Brevard from the college parking lot," he remembered. "I had a map they gave us. We rode straight for a while and turned right on some street that started with M."

"Meridian?" Gina offered.

"That was it. Then we had about seven or eight blocks to go before we had to get on the stilts."

"Where was that plumbing van?" she asked.

Justin's jaw dropped open. "Brevard," he said. "It was on Brevard!"

"Are you sure?"

He nodded. "I know it was Brevard because just after we passed the van Robbie remembered he needed a picture of himself on the trike. So I—"

Suddenly he wriggled out of his backpack and started pawing through it. "That plumbing van. I think I got a picture of it." He found the packet of photos, opened it, and began shuffling through the pictures. "Yeah, here it is. Two shots of it."

The other two kids crowded around to look.

"That's it," Tony said. "It has the name of the plumber on the side."

"Coffman," Justin said. In the picture's foreground was a grinning Robbie, but behind him was the van. It was a light-brown color, almost a tan, with two aluminum ladders on a rack at the top.

"Let's take this picture to the house it was parked closest to," Gina said, "and ask them if they called the plumbers. If they did, Coffman Plumbing is innocent. If they didn't, we get Dad on this."

"Maybe that wasn't the house that was robbed," Tony said.

"Well, we'll find out either way," she said. "Let's go."

"Hold on." Tony darted to the phone. "Let me check home messages." He dialed the Cogginses' voice mail number, then keyed in a password and a few more keystrokes and listened.

"No!" he yelped. He pushed "1" again to start it from the beginning.

"What is it?" Gina demanded.

"Quiet!" he hissed, clapping a hand to his free ear.

"Let me listen," she said, staring at his horrified face.

Eventually Justin got to hear it too.

"Message received at one . . . forty . . . two . . .

p.m.," intoned a computerized voice. Then the faint, crackly voice of Prof. McAndry said, "This message is for Tony." There was a loud buzz, which quickly faded. "Tony, I don't know how much battery I have left. I need you to call the college custodian and get the name of the person who painted the lighthouse."

The sound went dead for a moment, and Justin started to hand the phone back to Tony.

"Wait, there's more," Tony said.

The sound came on again halfway through her next sentence. "—let you know that there's been some vandalism here. Someone broke into the lighthouse and sprayed black paint all over the museum room. They broke a pane of glass in the *Republic's* display case. So get hold of Alex Chalmers at custodial and get the name of the painter. Tell him that to cover up the black spray paint, the museum room will likely need at least two coats of the cream-white paint he used earlier. Have Alex leave a message on my phone when he gets hold of the man and finds out when he can do this. I can take him over in my boat."

Tony's face had gone whiter than usual. Gina ran to her dad's study and brought back the campus phone list.

"Calm down, Tony," she said. "Don't get sick over this. It's just some stupid teenagers or something."

"Not the Spooks?" he asked as he dialed the college custodial department.

Gina looked questioningly at Justin.

"I doubt it," he said. "The Spooks haven't vandalized places. They don't want to mess things up—they want *stuff.*"

"That's what I think," Gina agreed.

"Hello?" Tony said into the phone. "Is this Mr. Chalmers? . . . Well, could you find him or page him? Prof. McAndry called and wanted me to get hold of him. Yes, it's an emergency. OK, I'll hold." He kept the phone to his ear, but put his hand over the mouthpiece. "We've got to get out to the lighthouse," he said.

Justin asked, "Do you think they got into your room?"

Tony smiled faintly. "Not a chance. It's too secure."

"How do you know?"

"Hello?" Tony said into the phone. "Yes, I'm being helped. I'm holding for Mr. Chalmers in custodial." He put his hand over the mouthpiece again and said, "Prof. McAndry's grandfather was a man who liked to do things right. The door to my room out there looks like wood, but it's got a solid steel core. The hasp is made of really hard steel and the padlock is uncuttable. So if anybody went out there hoping to break in, they could pry all day with a crowbar with no luck. They'd have to go away and come back later with a lot of high-powered equipment. Maybe even explosives."

"Do you have anything valuable out there?" Justin asked.

"A year's supply of zwieback," said Gina solemnly.

Tony glared at her and was about to say something when his expression changed. "Hello? Is this Mr. Chalmers?" He quickly repeated Prof. McAndry's message and wrote some things down on a piece of paper by the phone. "Thanks a lot," he said. "I'll tell her." With that he hung up.

The boy stared bleakly at the other two kids. "What else can go wrong?" he asked. "This is a disaster. The guy who did the painting this summer was a student, and Mr. Chalmers doesn't know if he's attending college this fall. He said he'd try to find him, but meanwhile he'll figure out a backup plan." Tony sighed. "Ready for another long walk?"

"Can't you call her back?" Gina asked.

Her brother shook his head. "Even if she's got enough battery to talk with, there's not enough to ring her phone. Anyway, I want to check out my room just to make sure."

They rode their bikes to the same parking lot where Justin had waited for Robbie to complete his canoe trip. Padlocking the bikes to a rack, they began the trek to the lighthouse.

Nine

The Bomb Plotter

Along the way Justin noticed Tony occasionally glancing back with a worried look. "Why does Tony keep doing that?" he asked Gina.

"He does that every once in a while, especially when he's under stress," she said in a lowered voice.

"Does he think he's being followed?"

Gina shook her head. "No; believe it or not, he's looking back to make sure we're still here. Remember, Tony thinks the rapture can happen at any minute."

Justin's eyes widened. "You mean he really thinks that we could vanish, just like that?"

"Yep. And all he would see when he looked back would be two little piles of clothing and some pairs of shoes." She stared at her brother's back and shook her head. "What a lonely feeling that must be."

"Gina, we're going to have to have a talk with him."

She glanced at him. "It sounds like a good idea, but I don't know exactly what to say."

"Look, I've been checking out the rapture idea, and I've got some serious questions about it."

"Really?"

"Yeah. I think it's going to be a whole lot different than Tony thinks it is."

"Well, go for it if you think you can straighten him out," Gina encouraged.

They found Prof. McAndry in the museum room holding a can of white paint and dabbing at the walls.

"Hi, guys," she said, surprised. "Did you try to call me back? Sorry I let my cell phone battery get low again."

Tony quickly told her what Alex Chalmers had said. "Anything else we can do out here?" he asked.

She glanced around. "No, nothing's really broken except the pane of glass from the case, and I cleaned that up."

"What about up in the light tower?"

She gasped. "I didn't even think of that. Would you go check?"

"Sure." The three kids ran to the corner of the room and started up the circular iron staircase. As they rounded the curve, they peered anxiously at the small door to Tony's room.

"It's secure," Tony said after checking the padlock.

"And no marks, either," said Justin after

carefully examining the hasp and doorframe. "They must not have come up even this far."

"Or they ignored it on their way upstairs," Tony added. "Come on!"

At the top of the stairs they found themselves in a small circular room totally enclosed by glass. In the center was something that looked like a large glass jar turned upside down. Inside was a glowing light bulb about four times larger than a regular household bulb. Rotating slowly around it was a curved reflector.

"This doesn't seem all that bright," Justin commented. "It's not a very big bulb."

Tony smiled faintly. "It doesn't have to be really bright," he said. "The reflector helps magnify it. At night, when it's pitch-black and there's no other light around, it's all you need."

Gina had slipped out onto the balcony, which ran around the whole top of the tower and was guarded by a railing. Beyond her, Justin could see the Port Bradley area, with the silver and glass towers of the college soaring over the rest of the town.

"Nothing damaged out here," Gina called.

Tony let out a sigh of relief. "That's good news," he said, and started down the stairs. "I want to stop off at my room before we go back home. I need to plot bombings."

Justin felt the hair just above his ears actually

rise upward. He slowed to a stop, while Tony continued clomping down the stairs.

"Gina," Justin whispered back over his shoulder, "Tony just told me he's going to plot some bombings!"

She cocked her head sideways. *"Plot bombings?* You heard him wrong."

"No, that's what he said."

"No way. Tony doesn't want to bomb anybody." She slipped past him on the stairs. "Let's go see what he's doing."

Gina entered the tiny room first, and Justin peered cautiously around the doorframe. Tony was standing with his back to them, facing one of his large maps of Israel, making two careful red dots on it.

"What are you doing, Tony?" Gina asked.

"That's about as close as I can get," the boy said thoughtfully.

Gina glanced back at Justin and shrugged.

Justin sighed with relief. He mouthed the words *It's OK.*

The girl gave Justin a puzzled frown, and he beckoned her outside the door and out of Tony's sight.

"It's OK," he whispered. "I know what he means. He's plotting the Palestinian bombings on a map."

Suddenly a terrified screech came from inside the room. "Gina! Justin!"

They hurried around the doorframe and into the room again to find a wild-eyed Tony whirling in circles. He lunged at the small porthole window and peered out. "Help! Gina! Justin! Where are you?"

Ten

Justin Jumps In

"Tony, cut it out," said Gina quietly. "Everything is OK. We're still here."

The distraught boy whirled and stared, then ran to her and grabbed her by the shoulders. "You're still here, you're still here," he babbled. "And you"—he grabbed Justin by the wrist—"you're still here too." Suddenly he collapsed to his knees, covered his face in his hands, and burst into a flood of tears.

"Should I get Prof. McAndry?" Justin asked Gina.

Tony stopped crying and looked up with wet horror in his eyes. "No, no . . . please don't get her. I'm OK. I just—"

"Is everything all right up there?" came Prof. McAndry's voice from below.

Justin hurried to the door. "Everything's OK," he called out. "I think Gina and I must have scared Tony or something."

"All right," she said doubtfully.

Gina reached out and swung the heavy door shut.

"Lock it," Tony quavered.

"No, I'm *not* locking it," she said.

"Don't go," he begged her. "Both of you stay right here."

"Tony," his sister said again, as though she'd been through this before, "Jesus loves you."

"I know, I know He does."

"You thought we'd been raptured, right?" she asked gently.

He gave a half sob. "Yeah, I did."

"Well, we weren't. See? We're both right here."

Justin cleared his throat. "Tony, can I ask you something?"

Tony stared at him. "Yeah." He swallowed. "Yeah, go ahead, Justin."

"How much sleep are you getting at night?"

Tony's eyes fell. "Not much, I guess."

"How much?"

"I—I get up at 4:00 to go through my prayer list."

"And what time do you get to bed?"

"Eleven, maybe 11:30."

"Midnight," Gina corrected him firmly, "or later, if you get a good Israeli shortwave station."

"Yeah, sometimes," Tony said, nodding humbly.

"And you're not eating right, either," she told him firmly.

Justin took a slow, deep breath and glanced at Gina. She gazed back at him helplessly.

"Tony," he finally said, "may I borrow your Bible, the one beside the laptop?"

Tony didn't answer for five seconds. Then he said, "Yeah. Why?"

"I want to read some texts to you."

"I'm OK, Justin. I just—had a little 'moment' there."

Justin reached into his pocket and brought out a piece of paper. "I'd still like to read some texts to you."

"What about?"

"The Second Coming."

Tony's head snapped up. "Why? I know them already. All of them."

"Let me just read them to you."

Tony shot an annoyed glance at Gina. "But why?"

"I've just got this little list of texts," Justin said patiently, "and they really encouraged me. I think they'll encourage you, too."

"I'm encouraged already," Tony said abruptly.

Gina punched him gently on the shoulder. "Tony, you just sit there and listen. It'll do you good."

Tony said nothing, but his eyes and mouth got very firm.

Justin looked at his list and flipped some Bible pages. Then he began to read, slowly and thoughtfully.

"'Do not let your hearts be troubled,'" he read.

"OK, I won't," Tony said.

"That wasn't Justin saying that to you, Tony," Gina said. "That was the Bible."

"I *know* it was the Bible."

"'Trust in God,'" Justin continued, "'trust also in me.' That's Jesus talking," he explained.

"I know," Tony said.

"'In my Father's house are many rooms,'" Justin continued.

"Lots bigger than this one," Gina giggled. Tony smiled faintly.

"'If it were not so, I would have told you. I am going there to prepare a place for you. And if I go and prepare a place for you, I will come back and take you to be with me that you also may be where I am.'"

Tony gave a deep sigh. "That's what I've been waiting for," he said.

Justin flipped some more pages and began to read again.

"'After he said this, he was taken up before their very eyes, and a cloud hid him from their sight.'"

Tony glanced up. "Where's that in the Bible?"

"In the first chapter of Acts," Justin replied.

"But what's that about a cloud? I knew Jesus went up, but I didn't remember the cloud. That's what it says?"

Justin nodded and kept reading. "'They were looking intently up into the sky as he was going, when suddenly two men dressed in white stood beside them.'"

"I've always wanted to see my guardian angel," Tony said.

"You will, Tony," Gina reassured him.

Justin continued reading. "'Men of Galilee,' they said, 'why do you stand here looking into the sky? This same Jesus, who has been taken from you into heaven, will come back in the same way you have seen him go into heaven.'"

Gina looked up alertly. "The *same* way?"

"That's what it says." Justin held out the open Bible to her.

"No, I believe you," she said. "But that sounds too—simple."

Justin glanced at Tony. Tony was staring steadily at a complicated chart taped to the wall. Justin thumbed some more pages.

"'Yes, it is as you say,' Jesus replied. 'But I say to all of you: In the future you will see the Son of Man sitting at the right hand of the Mighty One and coming on the clouds of heaven.'"

Gina grinned. "There are those clouds again. He went up in clouds, and He's coming back in clouds."

Tony nodded cautiously.

"'At that time the sign of the Son of Man will

appear in the sky,'" Justin read, "'and all the nations of the earth will mourn.'"

Gina reached over and put her hand on Tony's arm. He didn't move, but kept his eyes locked on his chart.

"'They will see the Son of Man coming on the clouds of the sky, with power and great glory. And he will send his angels with a loud trumpet call, and they will gather his elect from the four winds, from one end of the heavens to the other.'"

Tony glanced quickly at Justin, and then back to the wall. Justin flipped pages again.

"'Listen, I tell you a mystery,'" Justin read. "'We will not all sleep, but we will all be changed—in a flash, in the twinkling of an eye—'"

"That's the rapture!" Tony cried.

"'—at the last trumpet,'" Justin continued. "'For the trumpet will sound, the—'"

"Wait," Gina said. "I'm getting confused. That can't be the rapture. The rapture is quiet. People just vanish. And *then* the noise starts. Planes crash, cars crash, people start screaming for their loved ones. But Justin just read about a trumpet."

Tony took a breath through his nose. "It's the rapture," he said. "I'm telling you, that's a rapture text!"

"But what about the trumpet?" Gina asked. "A trumpet's not quiet."

"This one is," her brother said. "The righteous hear it; the sinners don't."

"How do you know?" she demanded. "The verse doesn't say that. It just says that the trumpet sounds."

"I don't know the answer to that," Tony confessed. "But trust me, it's a rapture text."

"You're the Bible-thumper," she said. "But which should I trust—you or the Bible?"

Tony said, "Well, the Bible, but—"

"Listen to me, smart guy," she said. "Since when does God blow a silent trumpet?"

"What are you talking about?"

She grabbed the Bible from Justin and turned to Exodus. "I just thought of something. Now, where is that text? Here it is. Listen up, Tony. This is where God comes down on Mount Sinai to give the Ten Commandments to the Israelites: 'Mount Sinai was covered with smoke, because the Lord descended on it in fire. The smoke billowed up from it like smoke from a furnace, the whole mountain trembled violently, and the sound of the trumpet grew louder and louder.' "

She handed the Bible back to Justin. "See? That's another time God blew a trumpet. Was it silent? No. Then tell me why the Second Coming trumpet would be a silent one."

Tony remained silent, shaken to the core.

Eleven

A Big Boxy Clue

Tony blinked a couple of times. "But Pastor Dave says—"

"Stop," she said. "You can't get on the Internet out here. It's just you and me and Justin and that Bible of yours. And that's all Pastor Dave has, too. Remember how he used to tell us, 'Read your Bibles, Christians, read your Bibles. Stand on the Word!'"

Justin said tactfully, "Maybe I should go on?"

"Yeah, keep reading," Gina agreed.

Justin turned to where he'd left off. "'For the trumpet will sound, the dead will be raised imperishable, and we will be changed.'" Then he turned some more pages. "'According to the Lord's own word, we tell you that we who are still alive, who are left till the coming of the Lord, will certainly not precede those who have fallen asleep. For the Lord himself will come down from heaven, with a loud command, with the voice of the archangel and with the trumpet call of God—'"

"Tony, are you listening?" Gina interrupted. "Justin just read about *three* loud things, not just one. There's a loud command, the voice of the archangel, and that trumpet again."

"'—and the dead in Christ will rise first,'" Justin continued. "'After that, we who are still alive and are left will be caught up together with them in the clouds to meet the Lord in the air. And so we will be with the Lord forever.'"

"The clouds again," Gina said.

"Just one more text," Justin said. "'For as lightning that comes from the east is visible even in the west, so will be the coming of the Son of Man.'"

"Tony," Gina said, "where do you get the idea that the rapture is going to be quiet?"

"Well, there are going to be *two* comings," Tony said. "The first is the rapture. It's going to be secret. The second is the loud one, the bright one."

Gina grabbed the Bible again and plopped it in her brother's lap. "Find the text."

"Find what text?"

"The text that says there will be two comings, a quiet one and a loud one."

"Well, there's no text that says exactly that," he said. "It's more complicated than that."

"It's got to be simple for me. I don't have a complicated mind."

"That's for sure."

Gina gave her brother a swift kick in the leg,

and he yelped. "Keep it simple," she said. "Those cloud-and-trumpet-and-lightning texts are simple."

Tony rolled his shoulders. "When we get back home I'll get on Pastor Dave's Web site and show you what the rapture's all about."

Gina shook her head. "You can't, because the Spooks stole our computer."

"Dad said he's bringing his laptop home from his office."

"Who cares about the laptop?" she sputtered. "I just heard the Bible tell me about the rapture, and it's not secret."

Tony glanced at his watch. "Whoa, it's suppertime."

Gina grinned at him. "I say we just stay here and chew on some nourishing zwieback."

Tony grabbed for his sister's hair.

"Justin, protect me!" she squealed.

They descended the circular staircase to find the professor putting some final touches on her paint job.

"Hi," she said. "Are you sure everything's OK? I heard some screaming up there."

"We're fine," Gina said.

Tony gasped. "You've been painting all this time? I should have come down here and helped you!"

"That's all right," she said. "I think I've got the

graffiti covered enough so that when the painter comes he'll just have to do one coat. Are you heading for the mainland?"

"Yes," Tony said.

"Come with me in the boat," she said. "This time I remembered to stash enough life jackets in it. Let's go."

As the little boat thumped across the waves, Justin glanced at Tony. *What's he thinking?* he wondered. *About the Second Coming? About the love of Jesus?*

Suddenly another thought came to him.

"Prof. McAndry," he said, "may I ask you something?"

She glanced around. "Go right ahead."

"Remember back at your house when you said you hoped the Cogginses' car was feeling better?"

She nodded.

"What did you mean by that?" he asked.

Tony said, "She meant that our Toyota is running rough. Dad's going to get it tuned up."

Prof. McAndry shook her head. "That wasn't exactly what I meant, but I'm glad you got it fixed."

"But it hasn't been fixed yet," Tony said.

"Do you mean that the Auto Troubleshooters didn't find the problem?"

Tony looked bewildered. "Auto Troubleshooters?"

"I saw the Auto Troubleshooters van in your driveway."

Suddenly she was being stared at by three pairs of very wide-open eyes. It startled her so much that she jerked the tiller and nearly spilled her passengers over the side.

"Prof. McAndry," Gina said in a numb-sounding voice, "when was this?"

"When was what?"

"When you saw the Auto Troubleshooters."

The professor paused. "Let's see. It must have been—yes, it was yesterday."

"What time?" asked Tony.

"In the morning," said the professor. "It was late morning, just before noon. But what's wrong? Is something the matter?"

Justin got out his black notebook and a pencil. "And what did you say the name was?"

"Auto Troubleshooters."

Gina poked Tony. "Dad didn't call anybody to work on the Toyota, did he?"

Tony shook his head.

Prof. McAndry smiled in a dazed way. "There's some mistake," she said. "They were there. Their van was backed right up close to the garage. They'd jacked up the front of the car and someone was rolling around under it on one of those little boards with wheels."

"You say it was a van?" Justin asked. "What color was it?"

The professor shut her eyes to think, but then suddenly remembered she was operating a boat and quickly opened them again. "Some sort of *vague* color," she said. "I remember thinking that the vehicle needed a more dramatic color if the company wanted people to remember it."

Tony and Gina both opened their mouths, but Justin spoke first. "Don't give her any clues," he said hastily. "Prof. McAndry, can you try again to remember the exact color?"

"It was the color of champagne," she said.

The kids looked at one another in bewilderment. "What color is champagne?" Gina wanted to know.

Prof. McAndry chuckled. "Good. I'm glad you children don't know. The color I'm thinking of is a very light tan, almost a beige."

The kids exchanged glances. Tony said, "But the other van was—"

Justin clapped his hand over Tony's mouth. "Wait, Tony." He handed the professor his notebook. "If Tony steers the boat, could you please draw the van you saw, along with the sign?"

"Well, I suppose so." She slowed the motor and let Tony guide the little boat. Taking the notebook, she carefully drew a picture of a boxy-looking van. On the side she made a square and wrote "Auto Troubleshooters" in the box.

"Why the square?" Justin asked.

"The square was white," she said. "It was a different color than the van itself."

Justin paused, then said, "OK, now let me show *you* a picture." Fumbling in his backpack, he brought out his packet of photos. Selecting one of the snapshots he'd taken on Brevard Street, he casually placed his thumb over the "Coffman Plumbing" sign and showed it to her.

Prof. McAndry nodded. "That's the one. It looked just like that."

He removed his thumb.

She stared at the sign. "Wait. I guess that's not the Auto Troubleshooters van after all."

"But the only difference is that the van you saw had a white sign?"

"Yes, I think so."

"Maybe there's more than one van," Gina suggested.

"Or it could be a magnetic sign," Tony suddenly said, "like the magnetic signs our church uses. They say 'Church Bus' on them, and you can stick them on any ordinary van when you pick up people, and then take them off during the week."

"But why is all this so important?" Prof. McAndry asked.

Gina stared at her. "Didn't you know?"

"Didn't I know what?"

"Our house. It was robbed by the Spooks yesterday."

The professor's mouth fell open. "Gina! Nobody told me!"

As Gina finished telling her the sad story, Prof. McAndry guided the little boat to the mainland dock. After saying their goodbyes, the three kids mounted their bikes.

"Patrol time," Gina said.

Justin nodded. "Let's go find that van."

"It's just going to get darker," Tony said. "And I'm hungry."

So they stopped at a sub shop, pooled their money, and shared some food.

"Let's go," Justin said after they'd finished their meal.

"Let's remember to stick together," Tony said. "If we find the van, we get its license number and location and find a phone booth and call Dad. Or we could just follow the van."

Justin shook his head. "We wouldn't have much of a chance following it on bikes. Besides, whoever's driving it might spot us."

"Hold it," Gina said. "If they can change signs, maybe they can change license plates, too."

"I've got an idea," Justin said.

About 45 minutes later they found the van. It

was parked on a lonely street next to a house with no lights.

"That's it," Justin said as they rolled slowly past. "And the 'Coffman Plumbing' sign is on the side. It's still got all those ladders on top. That should have tipped us off right away. Why would a plumbing truck need that many ladders? A lot of them don't carry any. Somebody remember the license number."

Tony gave a soft whistle. "It doesn't have plates."

"None on the back either?"

"Nope." Tony's voice sharpened with excitement.

Around the corner they came to a stop.

"What do we do?" Gina asked. "They might be in the middle of a burglary right now."

"Wait right here," Justin said. He got off his bike and jogged back around the corner again. Tony and Gina, waiting, suddenly heard a sound like a smack, and then running footsteps. Justin appeared, and grabbed his bike.

"Let's go," he hissed. "Now!"

Soon they were blocks away, still glancing fearfully behind them. It wasn't until they'd maneuvered their bikes into the Cogginses' driveway and around the Toyota and the SUV that any of them had the breath to speak.

"What did you do, Justin?" Tony asked, still short of breath from the intense bike ride.

"Yeah," Gina wanted to know. "What was that sound?"

"Wait," Justin said. "Let's go talk to your dad."

As soon as Austin Coggins heard some details and learned about the van, he called a friend on the police force. Soon they saw several police cars blink past their house.

"Too bad you guys didn't have a cell phone," he said. "I would have had half the force over there in 90 seconds flat." Five more minutes, and the phone rang. Mr. Coggins picked it up and listened. "Thanks," he said, and hung up.

"They're gone," he told the kids.

"We should have stayed and watched them," his son said sadly.

Mr. Coggins shook his head. "No, you did the right thing. With an operation as slick as that, they might have had lookouts. You're just lucky nothing happened. Only problem is," he continued, "is how to track them. They're probably constantly switching the signs on the side. And when they're not using the van, they've probably got it in a garage."

Tony said, "It's too tall for a regular garage."

"It could be kept in a warehouse," his father pointed out, "or maybe in somebody's back yard behind a fence." He paused. "How are we going to find that thing?"

"The *Bomber,*" Justin said, and immediately bit his lip. Very hard.

Mr. Coggins' eyes grew very wide. A huge grin spread across his bearded face. "Aha!" he said, like Dracula enjoying a tour of a local blood bank. "Exactly right! Tomorrow you ride with me in zee *Bomber!* However," he said in his normal voice, "it's going to be tough. From a half-mile up, one light-colored van is going to look pretty much like another."

"Not this one," Justin said.

Mr. Coggins glanced at him. "How so?"

"Because just after we spotted the van tonight, I ran back to it and pulled off one of its signs. And I tossed it up on top, with the magnetic side down. I doubt any of the burglars will think to look for it up there."

Mr. Coggins stared. "You little rascal."

Justin grinned. "So now all you have to do is to fly around and look for a van with a white square on top."

Mr. Coggins gave a grin of his own. "Me? What do you mean, *me?* How about *us?"*

"Come on, Justin," Tony said.

"You can do it, Justin," Gina insisted. "I go up in the *Bomber,* and I'm a girl. Are you telling me you can't do something a girl can do?"

That night Justin had a horrible nightmare. In it he was flying in Mr. Coggins' *Bomber.* His seat belt was loose, and the man had gone into a dive, and Justin was flopping around the cabin.

Twelve

Pastor Dave and the Truth

"Everything out of your pockets, Justin," Austin Coggins said the next morning. "I'll put them in this safe. That's so when we're upside down your stuff won't fall out and get caught in the rudder cable." He inserted a cell phone into a zippered pocket in his own jacket.

The two stood just inside a hangar at the Port Bradley airport, about to board the *Bomber*. Justin licked his lips and stared at the tiny red biplane. It wasn't much longer than a car. *Can this thing really fly with two people in it?* he wondered.

He watched as Mr. Coggins slowly circled the plane, tugging on cables, wiggling flaps, testing controls, even draining a sample of gasoline to see if there was water in it.

"When you have petroleum problems in the air," the man said, "you can't pull over to the side of the road and stop. Now, here's your parachute." He handed Justin something that looked like a very flat pillow with straps, helped him buckle it tightly on, and pointed out the rip cord. "That parachute's also going to act like a cushion for you on your back," he said. "This plane isn't very 'body-friendly.' OK, now in you get."

"I'm riding in *front?"* Justin asked.

"That's right. Let me buckle you in." Mr. Coggins threaded belts around him and yanked them tighter and tighter until Justin couldn't move an inch. "And here's this." The man handed him a folded airsick bag. "Stick it under your leg. Sit on it, but use it if you have to."

Well, Justin thought, *I'm strapped in so tight that at least I won't flop around in the cabin.*

Soon the bearded man was in the seat behind him, lowering a clear plastic dome over their heads. The engine roared to life. Justin wore a pair of earphones and a headset microphone, which allowed pilot and passenger to communicate.

Mr. Coggins contacted the control tower and asked for permission to take off. He then began taxiing down the approachway in a slithery, side-to-side way. "I can't see directly in front of me," his voice crackled in Justin's ears. "The engine sticks up too high. So while I'm on the ground I have to go forward in S curves."

In a minute or two they were on the runway itself. The engine roared louder, the plane moved forward faster and faster, and suddenly there was nothing under them but air.

"Now here's the plan," Mr. Coggins crackled as trees and buildings whipped by them and then sank away below. "The first thing we do is look for the van. Who knows whether it's out in the open at all? It might be in someone's warehouse. If we spot it I'll call the police, and we'll make sure they get to it. And then," he chuckled, "we'll have ourselves some fun."

Justin's heart sank so low that it almost touched his stomach.

Surprisingly, though, Justin found that the *Bomber* really was fun to ride in. He was strapped in so tightly that he felt as if he were part of the plane. And in a way, he didn't feel that he was high off the ground. It was as if everything outside the plane were just a large total-surround movie.

Below them the town of Port Bradley spread itself, beautiful in the sunshine. Justin found the college with its tall buildings, and the granite ones in the center of campus. He saw Prof. McAndry's tiny house, and his eyes scanned the nearby streets looking for the Cogginses' home.

"See anything yet?" Mr. Coggins' voice crackled. "Remember, you're going to have to do most of the looking. I've got to fly this thing."

Justin began running his eyes the whole length of each street from the wrinkled harbor water to where the town became the country. He saw a few long boxes that he soon discovered were tractor-trailers. He saw things that looked like small bugs, which turned out to be motorcycles. He saw scores of cars crawling along.

And then, with a catch in his breath, he saw the van.

"Down there," he said.

"Where?" Mr. Coggins asked. "Do the clock face. Our nose is 12:00. Where's the van?"

"Uh—9:00. No, now it's 8:00."

The plane banked sharply to the left, and suddenly the town rose beside Justin's left shoulder. The change in position confused him, and he tried to get his bearings.

"The water," Mr. Coggins said. "Is it between us and the water?"

"I lost it," Justin said. "Wait—there it is! Now it's at 11:00."

Mr. Coggins chuckled. "Well, what do you know." Justin could hear the beeping of a cell phone being turned on. "Margaret? Is that you?" And then the man began repeating a lot of police code numbers. Then he said, "No, I can't tell you the address; I'm in my airplane. Looks like it might be Beech, maybe Beech and Third, or Oak and Third, right around there. Beige van, white magnetic signs on the sides, no plates. The signs might read 'Coffman Plumbing' or they might read 'Auto Troubleshooters' or maybe even something else. I think, Margaret my dear, that I'm watching the Spooks on another raid."

As Justin peered over the *Bomber's* side, he

suddenly saw the lights of three separate police cars from different parts of the city begin to wink. Rapidly they crawled through the streets, approached the van with the tiny white square, and surrounded it.

"Wow! What a show, what a show," Mr. Coggins' voice crackled. "Nice work, Justin. Next time I call your daddy I'm gonna suggest that you get a super-huge Christmas present this year."

"I had a lot of help," Justin said into his microphone. "Gina and Tony and I worked together."

"Whatever. But thanks to you, the Spooks are probably history. By the way, speaking of show—get ready. We're heading out over the water, and I'm going to show you a couple of tricks. Let me know when you start feeling sweaty, and I'll stop. We don't want to get that airsick bag all yucky, do we?"

* * *

When they arrived back in the Cogginses' driveway, Gina and Tony dashed out the front door.

"Justin! Did you spot it? Did they catch them?" she shouted.

"We didn't hear any sirens," her brother said, "but I saw a police car with its lights on."

"And how was the flight?" Gina continued.

"Did you do the hammerhead? Did you fly upside down?"

Justin took a deep and cautious breath before he answered. "We did both, and lots more. It was kinda like watching a big movie. First the sky was on top of us, and then the water." He swallowed. "It was lots of fun."

"The Spooks," Tony said impatiently. "Did they get them?"

Justin nodded, and suddenly decided he would not nod again for the rest of the day. "We saw three police cars surround the van. I hope it was the Spooks."

Tony nodded grimly and held up a piece of paper. "I've got an interesting story to tell you," he said.

"Wait, wait, wait," Austin Coggins said. "Let's tell stories later, especially after I get a report from Mike and the rest of the gang at the station. We need to get something to eat. What do you kids like?"

"Mongolian Grill," said Tony and Gina promptly.

"Justin? What about you?"

Justin looked so thoughtful that Tony and Gina began to laugh.

"What's the matter, Justin?" Tony said, punching him softly on the shoulder. "Not hungry for some reason?"

Justin grinned weakly.

"Tofu," Mr. Coggins said. "We'll have the Grill people fix you up with a little bland plate of tofu. Or would that make you sicker?"

"I'll be OK," Justin said. "Let's go."

On the way to the restaurant Mr. Coggins dialed police headquarters on his cell phone and did a lot of listening. The more he listened, the wider he smiled. Finally he pushed the End button and put the cell phone back in his pocket.

"Kids," he said, "today you shall eat up. You deserve the thanks of the city."

Gathered in a cozy corner booth at the Grill, the four of them began fitting the pieces together.

"It was the Spooks, all right," Mr. Coggins said. "Once the police actually had people they could look at and fingerprints to compare, they knew who they were dealing with. A couple of them have records as long as my arm, and they're agreeing to cooperate. And the really good news is that most of the recent stolen goods are still in an old run-down warehouse they'd been renting."

"The *Republic?"* Tony asked anxiously.

"Mike said it's fine," said his father. "I didn't even have to ask about it. It seems that these people had connections with an online auction site something like eBay, only it was overseas. It's not a legal one, but a lot of wealthy people all over the world sign up for it to get great antiques and that kind of thing. Every once in a while the Spooks would send out a shipment of the best stuff and get big bucks in return."

"My dolls?" Gina asked.

"I don't know about that," her dad replied, "but they're probably there. Like I said, they haven't made a shipment for a week or two.

"And the vandalism at the lighthouse?" Tony inquired. "How does that tie in?"

"Apparently it doesn't," Mr. Coggins said. "Someone just wanted to make sure the police had enough to do, I suppose." He shook his head. "The one thing none of us have figured out is how the Spooks found out people wouldn't be home. None of the thieves have told them that."

"Um, Dad, I think *I* know the answer to that." Tony held up the piece of paper he'd brought with him.

Mr. Coggins blinked. "You do?"

Tony nodded. "Listen to this. It's from Pastor Dave."

"You mean our pastor from before? Isn't he in England?"

"Right." Tony glanced quickly at Justin and looked away. "I had some questions about the—the rapture. I wanted to get my facts straight. So late last night I found a phone cord and hooked up Dad's laptop to the wall and e-mailed Pastor Dave. But"—and Tony leaned forward in excitement—"I didn't use the e-mail address on Pastor Dave's Web site. I just automatically went to his e-mail address in my address book. And this is what I got back."

Tony glanced down through the letter. "The first part is sort of like How are you and all that. But then this is what he wrote after that." Tony cleared his throat.

"Tony, I am very surprised to hear you talk about a Web site. When I left for seminary here in England, I closed out the site because I knew I would have no time to give it the attention it needed. You may remember that I wrote a farewell letter and posted it on the home page."

Tony looked up. "I remember that letter," he said, "and I was really sad. But the site never stopped. It kept on going. We all got e-mails from somebody we thought was Pastor Dave, saying that because he was in England now he would have to move the site to another domain. The person gave a new Web site address and a new e-mail address for Pastor Dave."

Justin said, "Tony, didn't you say that the Web site had suddenly gotten a whole lot more interesting?"

Tony nodded. "Now I know why."

Mr. Coggins had a doubtful look on his face. "OK, fine," he said. "But I still don't see what this has to do with the Spooks."

"Listen to this, Dad," Tony said. *"I would be very careful,"* the letter continued, *"to check out the Web site you have been corresponding with. If they are using my name without my permission, they're probably up to no good. One question I have is What sort of information are they asking you for?"*

"Wow," said Austin Coggins softly. "Oh, wow. What a scam. They wanted information from you, and to get you all worked up they fed you a lot of news about Israel and kept you in a panic about the rapture."

Tony nodded. "Dad," he said miserably, "I—and several other guys from church—have been sending out prayer requests with a lot of details in them. Like how so-and-so is in the hospital and how somebody's aunt and uncle are going to travel to Europe and need prayers for their safety."

Gina hiccupped. "So that's how they knew when people would be gone!" she said. "It's a no-brainer."

"And," her father said, "if somebody saw the van, they'd think it was there for repairs. And it's such a blah-looking color that they'd forget about it anyway."

Gina nodded. "If the Spooks knew that someone was going to be gone to Europe, or even gone for a day, they would have all the time in the world to—" Suddenly she turned menacingly to

Tony. "Did you tell them that we were going to Uncle Pete's cabin?"

Tony nodded, his eyes down. "I—I told them everything," he confessed. "They told us on the site to include all the details so that everybody could pray more specifically."

"And you told them about Prof. McAndry, I'll bet."

"Everything. I wanted prayers for her so she'd be ready for the r—"

He paused, and a funny look came over his face. "Listen to this." He picked up Pastor Dave's e-mail again and kept on reading.

"You asked me about the secret rapture. Here at seminary they are urging us to do some really serious Bible study about the teachings we have always accepted. They reminded us that every Christian truth needs to be built on clear Bible texts rather than tradition or on ideas we bring with us to our study.

"I just wanted to let you know that there is quite a bit more to the subject of Jesus' return than I used to think. I haven't completed my studies yet. But Tony, I would encourage you simply to take your Bible and read the texts on Jesus' return and the events leading up to it. Just accept them as they read, because there and only there will you find the truth."

Gina looked at her brother and grinned. "Tony?"

"What, Gina?"

"I've got just one question for you."

"What's that?"

"What," she said slowly, "are you gonna do with all that zwieback?"

The three of them laughed so hard that people at other tables gave them funny looks.

"Hey," Justin said, "that stuff isn't too bad if you chew it long enough. In fact, that's what I probably need to take care of my stomach right now."

Again they laughed. And again they got funny looks from the other diners, but a few smiles, too.

Check 'Em Out for Yourself

Here are the texts Justin and Gina read in the lighthouse tower. They're all taken from the New International Version.

Exodus 19:18, 19
Matthew 24:27
Matthew 24:30, 31
Matthew 26:64
John 14:1-3
Acts 1:9-11
First Corinthians 15:51, 52
First Thessalonians 4:15-17